Check It Out!

Reading, Finding, Helping

by
Patricia Hubbell

illustrated by
Nancy Speir

Marshall Cavendish Children

Marshall Cavendish Corporation
99 White Plains Road, Tarrytown, NY 10591
www.marshallcavendish.us/kids

Library of Congress Cataloging-in-Publication Data
Hubbell, Patricia.
Check it out! : reading, finding, helping / by Patricia Hubbell;
illustrated by Nancy Speir. — 1st ed.
    p. cm.
Summary: Librarians love books, reading, and children and
inspire children with a love of books and reading.
ISBN 978-0-7614-5803-6
[1. Stories in rhyme. 2. Librarians—Fiction. 3. Books and
reading—Fiction.] I. Speir, Nancy, ill. II. Title.
PZ8.3.H848Ch 2011   [E]—dc22   2010018264

The illustrations were rendered with acrylic paint
on illustration board.

Book design by Vera Soki
Editor: Margery Cuyler

Printed in China (E)
First edition
1 3 5 6 4 2

mc **Marshall Cavendish**
Children

To all the wonderful librarians who inspire a love
of books and reading in children everywhere
—P.H.

To Otis and Stella
—N.S.

Books! Books! Books!
Our librarian loves books!

Curl-up-in-a-lap books.
Show-a-treasure-map books.

Books with pictures, books with none,

books about the moon and sun.

Little books, big books,

pirate books and pig books.

She keeps the books
on tables, racks—
and high and low on
shelves called stacks.

She knows just where to find each book,
is always glad to help us look.

A-F

Loves books of every age and shape.

She fixes books with glue and tape.

Straightens shelves, finds DVDs.
Finds books on snakes and bumblebees.

Gives out cards that we all need . . .

to take books home, and read and read!

She checks out books, helps fill our pack,

tells us when to bring books back.

CHECK OUT
DESK

**Plans book parties,
fixes snacks.**

Helps with schoolwork,
looks up facts.

Uses computers, reads reviews,

finds out what books are in the news.

She tells us how a book is made,
dresses up for Book Parade!

Shows us movies, old and new,

helps us when we cut and glue.

On winter days,
in cozy nooks,
she sings us songs
and reads us books.

When it's time to lock the door,
she goes right home and
reads some more!